FOR MR WOLF, WITH LOVE XXX

Starfish Bay® Children's Books
An imprint of Starfish Bay Publishing
www.starfishbaypublishing.com

ARTURO

© Hannah Beech, 2020
ISBN 978-1-76036-087-0
First Published 2020
Printed in China

ARTURO

WRITTEN AND ILLUSTRATED
BY HANNAH BEECH

Arturo was an anteater
with a **BIG DREAM**...

He wanted to be **WORLD-FAMOUS!**

Arturo just LOVED being the centre of attention. Even if that meant being super naughty, extra cheeky or even a little bit... RUDE!

HOW RUDE!

EVERYONE warned him.

One Tuesday, around about lunchtime,
the wind DID change...

...and Arturo got
STUCK.

(He had been playing catch at the time.)

At first, everyone
was **VERY** concerned.

ANTBULANCE

They tried **REALLY** hard
to unstick him.

But soon, they got used to it.

And they began to think it was actually quite useful!

Arturo did **NOT** get used to it.

He **WASN'T** famous and he **WASN'T** the centre of attention.
He wasn't even having fun being extra cheeky and
a little bit rude anymore! He was **TOTALLY FED UP**.

Would he ever get unstuck?

All of a sudden, news of Arturo's STICKY SITUATION
started to travel. He went on chat shows...

...and got invited to
GLAMOROUS celebrity
shindigs!

THE SNOUT

EXCLUSIVE:
Arturo
tells all!

Journalists wrote news stories
about him, and the brainiest scientists
tried to explain his unusual condition.

He was even offered a BIG job in London...

EVERYONE LOVED HIM!

Being famous was THE BEST!

Wasn't it?

When winter arrived, the nights seemed to
get longer and darker and colder than before.

ARTURO WAS LONELY and he started
to wonder if he'd made a BIG MISTAKE.

'Maybe,' he thought, 'being a world-famous
anteater ISN'T that great after all...'

'MAYBE it would be   MORE fun...'